The Revisionist

For Rose

Fellow Flower!

love,

Miranda Flower Mellis

2010

Miranda Mellis

Best of luck
w/ writing
& life!

The Revisionist

© 2007 Miranda Mellis

ISBN 0-9770723-7-1

Cover design and images: Derek White

Published by Calamari Press, NY, NY

www.calamaripress.com

The Revisionist

My last assignment was to conduct surveillance of the weather and report that everything was fine.

They set me up in an abandoned lighthouse seven miles outside the city. The lighthouse stood in the center of a junkyard, atop a mound of mossy dirt. It was trumpet-shaped with inward sloping walls. A stack of old sewing machines and broken pianos surrounded the dump. Local kids jumped from piano to piano, stomping the sour keys. Dogs chased them, barking. From the tower I couldn't hear, but I could see the kids jumping and the dogs chasing, their jaws snapping open and shut in the barking maneuver.

With the latest surveillance technology at my disposal, it was difficult to stay focused on the weather. I was tempted to make my own observations, and I did.

Looking out of the lighthouse with the ED100, a telescope that delivers images free of chromatic aberration (thanks to the FPL-53 extra-low dispersion "ED" optical glass in one of the two objective lens elements), I saw a family driving to the country on vacation. Behind them, a bomb went off. Through my headphones, I noted the rushing sound of radiation cruising low across the land. The father, who was driving, saw the mushroom cloud in his rearview mirror. The others didn't turn around, so they never noticed.

When they reached the campsite, the kids pitched a family tent. The father went inside, zipped up the flap door and wouldn't come out. "I need time alone," he called out.

His family sat frowning around the picnic table. The father was laughing and moaning inside the tent. The older sister shook her fists in his direction. The younger brother gave the tent the finger. The mother tore her straw hat off and stomped on it. She ground it into the dirt, right outside the flap door. The father heard the twisting feet of the mother. Coming out of the tent and seeing the hat on the ground, he said, "There's something I've got to tell you, but not in front of the kids."

The mother said, "Why don't you let them hear it too. We'd all like to know what you're doing in the tent."

"There's been a nuclear attack." Saying these words out loud had a strange effect on the father. He began running around and around in circles. Then he fainted.

The kids went inside the tent.

Through my telescope, survivors were running around in circles. Buildings were curdling. The very air had faded, was pixilated.

Inside one apartment building was an elderly woman. Her hearing aid was broken. She was watching the panic on television but could not understand what they were saying. She strained to hear them. She shook her head and wrung her hands. She kneeled and prayed. Her prayers exploded out of her mouth all over the carpet. She coughed up shards of bone and tiny blood-and-gristle soaked figurines. She washed the prayer viscera in the sink and hung them from a clothesline outside the window.

Upstairs from the old woman lived a blind man with a seeing-eye dog. This man, and subsequently his dog, was something of a renunciate. In every house the state had installed a radio and a television, which had to be on at all times. They could be turned down, but not off. Though the blind man could not see the television, his seeing-eye dog sometimes watched.

He didn't have a computer or phone. He had a welcome mat at the door, one blanket, and only the clothes he wore. He ate two small meals a day and drank water. He paced or sat contemplating.

The dog liked to stand by the open window, his snout to the wind, chin on the windowsill. Several times the seeing-eye dog looked right into my eyes.

The old woman left her apartment one day and collided with the seeing-eye dog in the narrow hallway between their apartments. He nudged her and barked. She watched how he opened and closed his jaw. She pointed at her ears and shook her head to say, "I can't hear." The dog looked at her, and she at him.

The seeing-eye dog walked around and around her legs. Her clothes unwound and floated into a spiraling vacuum above her head, created by the peregrinations of the seeing-eye dog. Her hair unfolded in a fan formation. Her pupils spilled open, submerging her retina in black ink. The seeing-eye dog continued his circumnavigations. The woman gradually floated into the air. She revolved in a tight catatonic orbit, forming the central axis of a wider concentric circle whose outer limit was delineated by the circling seeing-eye dog.

(eye)S ← → H(ear)

Back at the camp, the father gave the children tests. "What would you do in a nuclear holocaust?" But they couldn't answer. They pantomimed ducking under a school desk, but father frowned.

After they had quarantined the part of the county most affected by the bomb, I published a report showing that the radiation was harmless. My report on the radiation-less bomb was widely circulated. I was promoted.

They dispatched a tutor to upgrade my observational skills. He stayed at the lighthouse for a week and taught me remote viewing, sleepless sleep, and telepathy. He sat in the same chair all week, with his hands on his knees and his eyes open. I asked him about himself, but he would only discuss work. "Observe, record, propagate, disseminate," he said. "Do not reflect." He taught me to be very still, to look and listen. I practiced, recording analog, digital and telepathic data, and subsequently revising.

My employers wanted the real reports; I sent them the unrevised originals.

I struggled with static—mental noise that interfered with my ability to hear and see what was in front of me. The tutor told me that eventually the static would clear and then I would not need machines anymore.

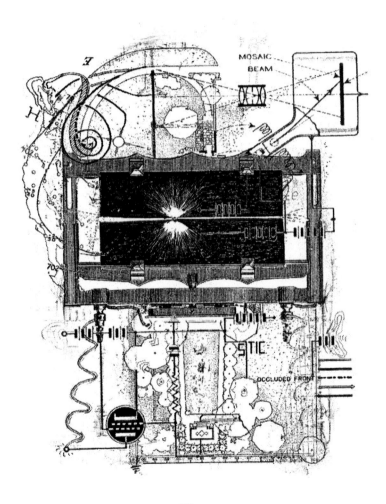

After my tutor left I resumed my personal surveillance habits, using the new technologies and practicing the skills of empathic-proprioception that the tutor had imparted. I could hear people's heartbeats. My own heartbeat could synch up with others' even over long distances.

A lot of people could see, by observing their own environments for themselves, that my reports were fraudulent. People wanted to get away. Escape schemes flourished. One guy made a pile of money selling plots on Start Over Island. I went there myself, at first on vacation, and then for real. They gave you a new identity, a clean slate.

It was the new expatriation. You got a giant eraser, like the ones from grade school, and just slid it over the past.

It wasn't just the radiation that made people flee to Start Over Island. They flocked to the island because the particulars of their lives had become meaningless. Their surfaces were covered with faded images, like old walls. It was tiring to climb over this wall every time there was a party, a run-in, or the required 'date.'

One had to show one's date a good time. It was not easy to do. The significance of the date slid around in people's minds. It was suspected that dates and death were somehow linked. It was normal to get to know people and then to be scared or hurt, even killed by them. And then, all the mutations... so they came.

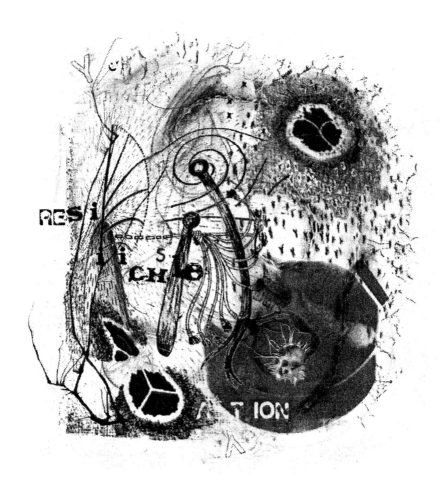

Anybody with any money moved to the island. There were mutant children who sensed the impending exodus of all the adults, who planned on leaving their monstrous children behind.

The mutated kids were impossible to soothe, perpetually hungry and thirsty, shivering and angry. The adults said, "It's only me going. The kids will get by. There are other adults around, social services, orphanages, hospitals, shelters. The others, they'll stick around, get pissed on the head by acid rain and all that, but I'll be gone, and the kids will just get used to it."

But the kids didn't get used to it, or forget, because it never occurred to them that they could. No one had ever suggested it.

One came to the island seeking a new identity, but found things the same as before. We pretended not to know each other. One walked past one's parents looking straight ahead, resisting the urge to accuse them of something. After the initial difficulty of pretending not to know anyone, soon we genuinely couldn't remember.

But there were side effects—reddened eyes and this compulsion to rip things. People would be talking mildly at the bank and suddenly rip out their own hair, or go outside and rip the moat of shrubbery surrounding the bank with their bared teeth. They would stumble through the parking lots, chewing the shrubs, eyes gyrating.

I soon returned to my revisions at the lighthouse. At least there I didn't have to pretend not to know anyone. I hardly ever saw people anyway. I saw them, but they never saw me. I might have stayed on the island if there was no one there I recognized. But there they all were, friends, acquaintances, family members.

At first I didn't mind—since we were now 'strangers,' I no longer had to do their dishes, take them to AA meetings, make sure they'd taken their pills, fight them off, go to counseling with them, worry about them, be jealous of them, suspect them of lying, miss them, hold their babies, take them to the hospital, help them move, fantasize about them, comment on their haircuts, see their points, admire their looks, proffer my goodwill, keep their secrets, pacify them, reassure them, seek their approval, recover from their abuses, read their manifestos, find them unreliable, try to see their good qualities, hope they'd vote, impress them, ignore their stupidity, or compete with them for jobs and housing.

One hoped that one could become someone else on the island. But the assumed identity eroded under pressure and health problems were insoluble. Everyone wanted to be free of the augur, the word, the sound, the image, and the omen of cancer—to be rid of pollution, hate, loneliness, fear and purposelessness. After the initial relief of moving to the island, one could not deny the persistence of the old life. One took a new name, a new everything, and still it dragged on, within.

I fled to Start Over Island hoping to be free of the pervasive sense of foreboding brought on by my profession and a lifetime of repressed violence, confused wanderings and relationships, and endless, exhausting tête-à-têtes.

Most of my friend's pets had grown old and stiff. One friend's dog required diapers. Several friends had quit drinking and smoking. The rest were preoccupied with trying to find free surfing classes or abandoned castles, and eluding creditors.

The day after I ripped my own mother's clothes off in a supermarket, I suspected I needed to leave Start Over Island. My last conversation there convinced me of it. I had been visited by a lady with razor-thin lips. She made astral killings her business. She sold "air art" on the side. "You have enemies here," she told me. Evidently, she had been hired to murder my astral body. Furthermore, she said she had already done it. Hadn't I noticed anything different?

Some others, feeling remorseful, had gone back. But they'd lost their authority over their mutant children who now did whatever they had to do, as well as whatever they could get away with.

I concentrated on taking measurements of the rising ocean, training my instruments on the creeping shoreline and tidal fluctuations, and revising my data to report, unaccordingly, that the sea was just as usual.

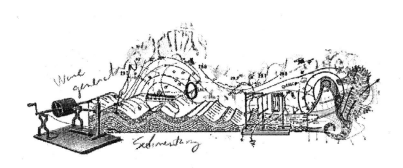

Nature will always be natural, the tutor had told me. For what is ever not natural? Even lies are just a kind of weather. We are not interested in little truths or perturbations. There are too many of them.

The ocean had always functioned as a kind of clock for the sentient, but gradually it stopped telling our kind of time. The ocean was, simply, not the ocean anymore in the usual sense of the word. It was onto other measures. It tossed up four hundred dead dolphins one day, and claimed one hundred thousand baby seals the next.

The place where one could now go to experience the ancient rhythms of nature was the convenience store. Convenience stores were becoming "nature," and nature had become a run-down, thrashing machine. In the convenience store, people howled and chirped at one another.

A man was voiding near the chips aisle of a convenience store. He was in the process of digging a hole with a jackhammer to bury his shit when a robbery took place. He pulled out his video camera and caught the event on tape. He couldn't wait to get home and show his family the video of the robbery in progress, which had interrupted the burial of his bowel movement.

I fabricated phenomena, makeovers for a bevy of new industry-spawned carcinogens:

- *the air is getting cleaner by the day*
- *cloud miasmas: the future is bright*
- *animal depressions: we're living longer than ever*
- *500 trillion nanobots, built an atom at a time, war in a suitcase*
- *carbon dioxide emissions from fossil fuel combustion have proven highly beneficial to life on earth, especially cockroaches and poison ivy.*

For three weeks straight I had been observing the ocean. On the twenty-first day I saw a man running along the shoreline. I could hear his feet hitting the sand. It was the first time I was able to discern with utter precision every nuance, every gearshift, every soft click of another person's mind.

He remembered he was there to run, and he even remembered a time there was a reason for it. He did not remember the reason, nor did he want to. He feared he might be running for the old reasons, and didn't want to imitate himself. That would be running in place. Not too far down below the top shelves of his memory he knew he was there to run for a reason, but still he decided to invent a different reason. He was reinvigorated by this decision to *find a new reason*, and ran even faster. He'd run seventeen miles when he realized in dismay that he'd forgotten to do it. He'd been running off the memory of an idea.

He was exhausted and his lungs burned. He pushed his head into the sand and his legs ran in a circle around his head that he was screwing into the sand. He pushed down and screw-drove himself until only his toes stuck out. His toes were twined around each other. I could no longer hear his thoughts. Was he dead? His heart was still beating.

Then I heard another heart beating, a smaller and quicker one. A girl was beachcombing towards him. She mistook his toes, twisted around each other in a spiral, for a shell. She knelt down to collect the shell. She yanked. It was the first time she ever had difficulty picking up a shell. "This must be some kind of seaweed," I heard her say aloud.

The girl had a Swiss army knife. There were a myriad of tools hidden inside the knife's slick red carapace, which unfolded like bug appendages at the joints. She selected the tiny perforated saw. She began to saw and realized the root of what she thought was either a seashell or seaweed was very deep. She snapped the saw blade back into the shaft and put the knife back in her pocket. She dug for the root of the stalk. "This is a long root," she said aloud. A dog came along and helped her dig. Soon they had dug out the entire seashell and she guessed it was the biggest conch ever.

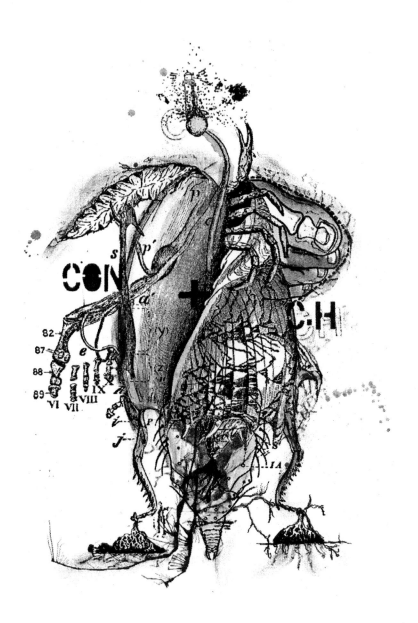

The conch made the Guinness Book of World Records. The girl won a special prize from her school because her discovery had been placed in the Guinness Book. How would she handle her newfound fame? She could take advantage of it to be cruel to people who bored her. She could lord it over everyone. She could pretend her discovery was no big deal. In the end, she felt the most honest thing to do was lord it over everyone.

The curators at the Big Conch Museum didn't appreciate her attitude. They argued, "This conch doesn't belong to you. The conch comes from nature."

"It wouldn't be here if I hadn't found it."

"Just because you find something doesn't mean it belongs to you."

"Then to whom does it belong?"

"It belongs to the Big Conch Museum."

"Why should it belong to the Big Conch Museum more than anyone else?"

The chief curator agreed and the girl took the conch home and put it in her room.

On the days I was too tired to work, I watched frigate birds hover in slow swooping circles over the dump, around and around the lighthouse. They would swoop right in front of my telescopes and cameras. I would be making an observation when the white patches of a frigate bird would fill up the lens.

I took to feeding them. I soon had a flock living with me. They perched on every available branch, rail, chair-back, bedpost, mirror-top, and my shoulders and head. They made soft noises—feather-flapping and fluffing, claw-stepping, and peck-grooming.

Sometimes people came to scavenge in the junkyard around the lighthouse, but they weren't aware of my presence.

There is a certain intuition that humans share. When one human has faked his or her own disappearance, or undergone astral death, or lied about radiation and global warming—no matter how long ago—other humans sense it. Humans are intuitive, that is their adaptation. Some call it spiritual, the way that intuitions intertwine, and knowingly billow around, like satellites, or squid.

One day, I made out a familiar heartbeat. The conch awakened to find he was leaning against the girl's bedroom wall. He was upside-down with his arms and legs wrapped around his body. He tilted his head and his body whipped apart and unraveled. His skin flew off and stuck to the walls.

When the girl came home, she suspected that the curator from the Big Conch Museum had come in and blown up her conch.

She hired a private investigator to follow the curator of the Big Conch Museum around. The PI had a long, fleecy, dirty beard down to his waist and a tight black suit. The PI discovered that the curator listened to dissonant music. He brought the girl along and they listened under his window. At first the curator was listening to Sam Shalabi's record *On Hashish*, dedicated to Walter Benjamin. "Sounds like he's experimenting with explosives," the girl whispered. Then the curator put on Sun Ra. The curator was singing along:

> *It's a nuclear war.*
> *Your ass gonna go.*
> *Watcha gonna do?*
> *Without your ass.*

The girl and the PI figured the curator was planning a nuclear attack. They ran in terror to a nuclear fallout shelter.

The old woman with the broken hearing aid was already there with the seeing-eye dog and the blind man, who were asleep. She offered the girl and the PI seats on milk crates covered in burlap. She put her kettle on a small propane stove. No one spoke. It had started to rain outside. The PI fell asleep. The girl didn't know whether she should go save the remains of the conch. She didn't want to run through the acid rain. She worried aloud about her dilemma, but the old woman couldn't hear and everyone else was asleep. The girl took out a notebook and drew pictures for the old woman, explaining about the conch. Once the old woman understood the girl's problem, she offered to go and get the conch. The girl wasn't sure if she should accept. But the old woman didn't mind a little acid rain. She was used to bad weather. She left, passing a steelyard on her way to the girl's house. There were kids playing games like jacks and h-o-r-s-e. The old woman stopped to watch a round of foursquare. Then she got caught up in a game of quarters, and forgot all about the conch.

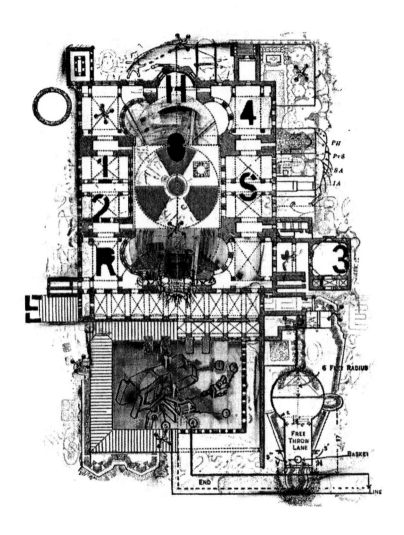

The girl worried that something had gone awry with the rescue mission since the old woman had not yet come back. Night fell, and the girl was tired. Everyone else was still asleep. The PI had wrapped his beard around his neck for warmth. The girl was sad and cold. She looked around for something warm and spotted the PI's beard. She took out her Swiss army knife, unhinged the tiny scissors, and carefully cut the PI's beard off at the throat. What was left of the beard sprung loose and fanned out like a bib below his mouth. She wrapped the beard hair around her own head and went to sleep.

When she woke up, everyone was gone. The girl walked outside. There was a storm. Her head was wrapped in the PI's fleecy, dirty beard, but she didn't care what anyone thought—she'd lost her conch to the curator's bomb. She walked through the rain, listening to incessant thunder. Her skin hung from her bones in the shape of despondency. Her head-wrap of fleecy beard-hair gave her an irresponsible look. Her clothes sagged. Her socks slid helplessly away from her feet. Even her underwear glissaded down like a dirty, abandoned wedding train behind her, drained of all proportion and propriety. All drooping, she slimed down the street like oil. She hated how everything had collapsed—without the helicoptering arms even, of drowning humans, or any of the fanfare associated with will—into the shape of what was nearby.

Desperately, the girl grabbed a bolt of lightning in her hand. The lightning made the beard hat fly off. An image of the conch came to her and she realized, because of the retrospective vision imparted by her being electrocuted, *that it had never been a conch.* She ran back to her room. Skin, organs, and body fluids were splattered all over the walls. She slowly pieced the runner back together. Her depression lifted as she sewed.

The runner had journeyed far from his original intention. He had been absorbed by the world and now he was a rag doll. What was left for him to fear?

The girl and the rag doll shared the camaraderie of two marooned astronauts, their salvation, at the last hour, catalyzed by a series of events whose effects may be described at once—without any temporal contradiction—as both predestined and accidental.

I met the curator at an outdoor exhibition of the astral-killer's air art. He gazed into my eyes and I invited him to come by the lighthouse.

The curator sat in the tutor's chair. He tapped his lips and tilted his oblong head. His voice was gauzy. His skin was opalescent. A filament of blood, like a creek, traversed one eyeball.

I offered him coffee. He didn't want coffee. I played Bartók, whale songs and Cypher in the Snow. He didn't want music. He asked me to change my clothes. He didn't like any of my clothing. He tried, unsuccessfully, to capture a frigate bird. He clawed his own face. He was jealous of my manner. He didn't like my personality, he said. He described me as a very realistic flashback.

It was Friday night, the traditional time to go to a show. In a daze, we wandered to the venue. As soon as the bands began to play, we turned spasmodic and insectivorous. It was a night that ended in a pile of countless similar nights. You could pathologize the repetition, call it futile, but if you considered the aesthetics of repetition as such, you might actually begin to embrace eternal recapitulation.

There was a couple at the club who were known for falling in and out of love with each other within seconds. They just kept dividing, reuniting, and subdividing in mitotic fashion, though they physically didn't replicate themselves. The curator and I fell into this pattern.

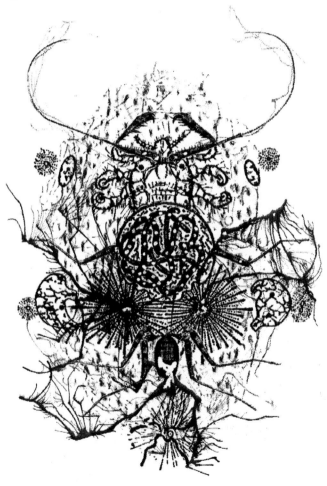

I was no stranger to the trade-off between mitotic love and life. As a child, my own mother told me the human heart spun on an axis smaller than a dime. Like her father, she sold "life for love" insurance. For the price of ten years off your life, you could purchase insurance on a ten-year love affair. Plans were also available in increments of twenty-five and fifty. If your love affair failed before your insurance expired, they'd provide you with a clone of the loved one for the duration of the term. Sometimes the clone worked out even better than the original.

My uncle had a beef with the whole concept of insurance. So my cousins put him into an assisted living home for his own security. There he claimed he saw people being pushed around at night in laundry carts. He witnessed seniors being turned into frigate birds and relocated to giant atriums. My uncle, who had refused to insure his love, whose nostrils were the size of circus tents, claimed that love clones were stored in the basement and actual relatives were housed in birdcages in the courtyard.

A reporter intercepted my uncle's rants and believed it was more than a conspiracy theory. She submitted her story: *Senior Citizens Being Turned into Frigate Birds and Replaced by Clones*. Her editor put her in the assisted living home, and she was turned into a frigate bird.

When we visited my uncle, he would always single out this one bird, saying it was the reporter.

One new arrival to the assisted living home, a centenarian, believed my uncle. The centenarian also detested the sheetrock toast they served and ran away to become a prostitute. A man paid her to show him her underwear. She lifted her dress. Under her skirt was outer space. There were children and babies dangling like ripe fruit from the joints and nooks of unfamiliar constellations. "You won't find the Big Dipper under there," she cackled, letting out a whooping laugh that sent the man running. But my uncle had been following her and was still watching. The centenarian opened her mouth wide. Down inside her mouth was a typewriter. The keys were her teeth and her tongue was a ribbon. Her bottom lip was the spacebar.

She was always looking for fresh material. The babies hanging from the stems in space between her legs wouldn't do. They had no life experience. My uncle courted her. When he lifted her skirt, an iguana came out.

"This music makes me home sick," the curator whined. The curator had stopped by the lighthouse. "Please change this music and take off your clothes and stop boiling water." We (the frigate birds and I) were tired of listening to him.

A blimp flew by trailing a "Manifest Destiny Soiree" banner. "What is the rationale for this?" I asked. The curator announced, "Uncle Columbus Reagan and Aunt Napoleon Thatcher are having a soiree and I am invited. I must go," he said, "but first . . ." And he shit on my floor. Then he wrote on my forehead with a marker, "Un-enjoyable." The frigate birds had seen enough. They swooped in and carried the curator off in their claws.

The prisons—already filled up with people who got caught with drugs, or had no job, or disagreed with the president, or had no health insurance—were expanded. Soon most of the population of the city was in prison and a few grinning white people floated around in the Manifest Destiny Soiree blimp surveying their property. Their grins floated around on their faces.

The people blamed each other for everything and in a trance colluded with the blimp soiree campaigners. One woman had only been given one second to speak, and what could she say in such a short amount of time? She used the second as well as she could. She opened her mouth and a tiny spider danced out. The spider essayed, *"On Mirrors"*:

"Mirrors should not be held accountable for the actions of just one mirror, or mirrors that have gone before. By the same token, the behavior of the mass of mirrors cannot help but affect one's perception of particular mirrors. I was raised to distrust mirrors and to keep my distance from them. While I have known some good mirrors, I've never wanted to get too close to one. Indeed, there are times when I feel hatred for a particular mirror, especially if it seems to be getting away with something, or being granted special dispensations, just because it's a mirror. I've tried to see beyond the mirror's appearance, to see some kind of essence beyond the mirror's façade. But this is difficult to do, because mirrors have a way of wanting it both ways. They want you to see beyond their façade, to appreciate them for qualities that transcend the fact of their mirror-ness, and at the same time, they want and expect all the privileges and pleasures that society grants mirrors. Indeed, a mark of their privilege is that they want to be seen as more than, even as exceptional despite, their privileged positions as mirrors. And yet, if I'm honest with myself, I can see that there are similarities between myself, and mirrors. No one wants to be judged on the basis of physical appearance alone. It takes a special kind of looking to see beyond form."

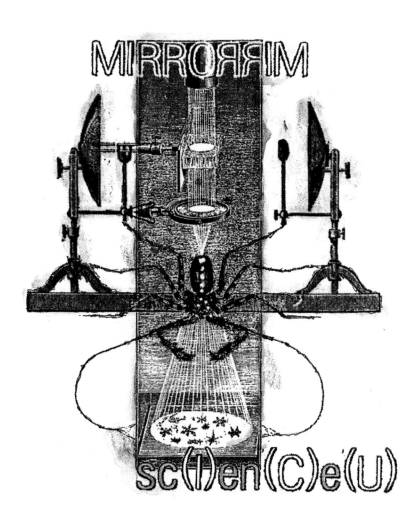

There were family photos, but it was difficult to know who the family had really been. One grandma had jumped out of many windows in her ongoing escapes. She was always running. The question that she ran with was constant. Book learning had been practical for her children, but it drove a wedge between she and they. They listened to her stories and could only imagine these stories as text and/or some form of either marketable or unmarketable object. The grandmother realized that in their minds, trauma was something to sell or forget. One child complained that her grandmother's stories held something back. Grandmother agreed that stories were not functioning the way they once had. "What about poetry," she said. The youngest wrote poems. There she found a way to include the historical reality and necessity of grandma's escapes intertwined with her own sense that (excepting madness) there was no place to escape to. The poem tried to say that the child's attempt to learn the strategies of assimilation was in conflict with atavistic rules of continuance. The problem was, as one man with a gun to his head said, "I am made to suffer more than is humanly necessary, and therefore it is difficult to care either way."

From the lighthouse I could see that the despisers of life had grabbed hold of the economy. Yet other economies erupted. I watched a young woman watching a Russian film. The phone rang when she arrived at home. A tangible force field emanated from the phone. She knew not to answer it. The next day, a packet came in the mail. She put it back, unopened, in the mailbox. It was now common knowledge that the future lurked in communication systems.

My phone rang. I refused to pick up because I didn't want to find out that it was not the future, which was (mathematically) the same as being the future so I picked up to find out. It was the woman who watched Russian films. She said, "Is this who I think it is?"

And I said, "Whom are you calling for?"

"You."

"Then yes."

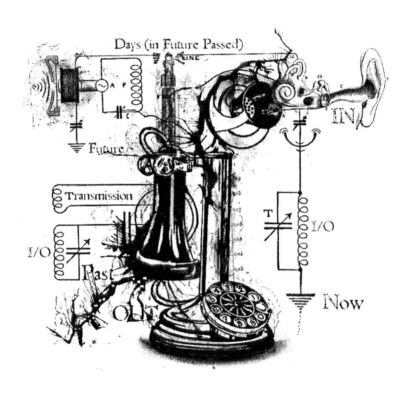

Days (in Future Passed)

Future

Transmission

I/O

Past

OUT

IN

T I/O

Now

The seeing-eye dog was giving a lecture called *A Corpse Ate Death*. There was an avant-garde orchestra accompanying his lecture. Dogs barked along, and small children played answering machines, recorders, trombones, triangles, and ukuleles. When I arrived, the seeing-eye dog was howling:

"With a pang I imagine you sobbing, kneeling, miserably grieving. I become sad at the thought and want to rescue you—from my imaginings. Perhaps it is necessary for you to mourn, the disappointment eternal, the balm expired. This too shall not pass, but instead, reoccur. It is not the moment that passes, but the body. Yet your feeling of desperation has nothing to do with that inevitability. It flares up of its own accord. Whether you are fur-covered, or metal-skinned, whether designed for running, predation, war, sex, speed, work, or space travel, the feeling, like a stain, remains..."

A frigate bird spoke. She described the world as fabric. The idea that nothing would ever be lost, the melancholy frigate bird said, still gripped the collective imagination, even as the fabric of the world wore away.

I turned my telescope and caught the image of a young man in a leaking boat. He used a Dixie cup to tirelessly bail out the water. It did not matter that his vessel was both small and full of holes; his tireless devotion kept him afloat.

In the center of the city I saw an artist fall in love with a statue. She stuffed the statue into the trunk of her black 1964 Buick Skylark in the middle of the night. But when she got home, there were ten people in the trunk, each one no longer than a finger. They all looked familiar. She saw that each was an aspect of the beloved statue, and that the statue had divided into the many small parts of itself. She placed them on her mantle. They assumed various postures, of threat, submission, kindness, boredom, desire, obsession, terror, disinterest, worship—now facing her, now turning away, theatrically contorting, sometimes falling deliberately into the fire from whence they screamed bloody murder and hurled epithets. But they did not die. Eventually they crawled back up onto the mantle and renewed their poses.

In the outskirts of the city, I saw a man lying on the floor of a dirty small room. There was nothing else in the room but a projecting movie and a chair. The movie showed him sleeping on the dirty floor. He sat in the chair and dissolved.

His daughter came home and found the bones of her father in the chair. She sat on his lap bones, and she turned to bone dust. Her son came in and lay on the floor. There was nothing else left but the movie of his grandfather sleeping on the dirty floor, the chair and the combined bones. He sat in his mother's lap bones and dissolved. His daughter came in and lay on the floor. There was nothing else left but the movie of her great-grandfather, the chair and the bones. She sat in her father's lap bones and she turned to dust.

I averted my eyes.

A gigantic tree fell out of the sky, crushing a truck at a nearby university and killing three students. Their skeletons crouched in there, bent under the tree. After an appropriate interval, they became a comedy act.

In the past, when something fell out of the sky, or there were collisions, men in jumpsuits arrived, sirens blaring, to erase all traces. Something was always done about something. Now nothing was done, except documentation. For every event, there were multiple documents and artifacts, until there were more documents and artifacts than events. Inevitably someone called a document an event, and people made documents of documents.

The old woman with the broken hearing aid stepped on a piece of glass and no blood came out. Her heart froze in fear and her body locked up. The PI had a special tool that he sidled and jimmied down into her. It was a pink forked tendon, tongue-like in the way it sought out dark holes. He vacuumed her eyebrow roots. Her eyelashes flaked off. All the hair on her body blew away as if she were a dandelion gone to seed.

She came from a long line of anxious people— depressives on one side, alcoholics on the other. Everyone in her family had been told that a walk on the beach would do them good. They were told to collect sand dollars and gull feathers. But when they got to the beach they were more depressed than ever. The walk on the beach proved to be the last straw. They ran away from each other. A few of them rushed into the sea, grateful to die.

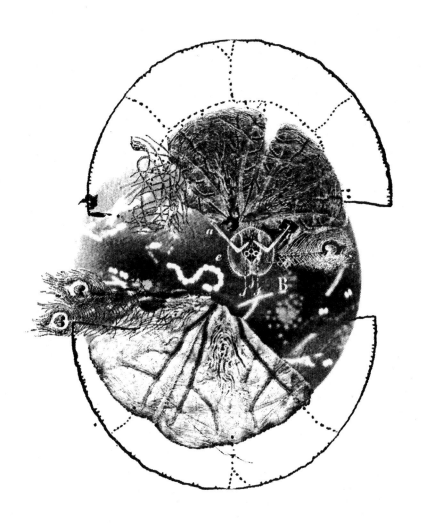

The girl who found the conch saw her father die. She had been standing across from him and waving. Before the accident she said, "He doesn't see me."

When she was outside in the world, she felt she was not as visible as when she was inside of her house. There she could see herself perfectly in the mirror. She could also sense her own outline. Her mouth moved and words came out. Yet this outline, and this mouth that moved were not exactly what she thought of as herself.

Her father often stood on the side of the highway doing his act. He had no control over himself. He stood there yelling at cars and waving his fists. He had moved to the city from far away. He gradually spent all of his time yelling at traffic. Noise assaulted him from every direction. The day she was waving, seeing that he did not see her, she watched him become the inside of a wreck. A flaying and screeching tidal wave of cars surged into him. The impact of the car crash caused him to explode. But where organs, blood, and tissue should have spattered the street, only a thousand shards of steel and boomerangs of plastic whirled. The debris circled the area where the man had once stood, flying, as though sentient, in formation into the sky.

Her father's head fell out of the sky and attached itself to the top of her head.

She played in the dump outside of the lighthouse, and her father's head turned this way and that.

The lighthouse had a little door that was making a sound. It wasn't open, and it wasn't closed. It just emanated noise, and she stood, with her two heads, and wondered what to do.

There were so many different kinds of time. There was time measured in objects and time measured in space. There was time enclosed by language and there was time splattered in the form of shipwrecks and galaxies. There was the way a person measures the distance between what she once felt and the moment she realizes she no longer feels that way. There was also the void, for which time was conventionally the foil.

The girl stood before the tiny cherry-colored door. She kicked it and came in. I kicked three giant jugs of water down the narrow, spiraling flight of stairs. The tumbling jugs made the sound of buoys colliding.

She evaded the water bottles and made it into my room. I admired her coat. Her mother had embroidered her coat thus: Everything/Depends/Upon Me. This was the mother's direct treatment of the thing.

We watched a swan float on the irradiated tides.

"It has babies," she said.

"Cygnets," I said.

"In the city," her father's head said, "I became obsessive."

After the curator, I got involved with a Valkyrie, who told me she would quit smoking on my behalf and showed me a contract. This contract was bullshit, but somehow it was also authentic. Valkyrie wanted to get into this business of documenting documents. She was no longer interested in anything 'original or spontaneous', such as sudden, organic shouts. She said she'd rather be 'a rigid glass skyscraper than a toady wet nurse.'

She posed, climbing a ladder, shooting a lawn with a .357. She took up marching to work. She goose-stepped, swinging her arms like scissors. The people minding the kiosks and hanging out in the doorways that lined her path to work found her forthright stomping amusing. If she lost her balance or deviated from her pattern she would stop and start over.

Even blood could no longer be counted on to spill. The lover would wait all day for a call, but when the phone rang she would not answer.

Characters were anybodies, strangers arrested in poses. Economic, ecological, and emotional problems formed a compass. One worked late into the night at something. Dreaming was considered a method for understanding something. Relationships were thought to lead to something.

There was a couple living down the hill from the lighthouse, a skinny bike messenger with a mohawk and a plump redhead with rolled-up jeans. They often sat, soundless, absorbing the antics of flat spacers, cans of beer in hand. They lived in a small room with low slanted ceilings. The old woman with the broken hearing aid, his mother, stayed with them often.

One day a great buckling wave of tarmac took their block by surprise. They naturally walked outside. He sat on a curb. She looked down at him. He looked at her and she looked at the stop sign on its side after the buckling wave of tarmac, and then the fog rolled in. He got cold then and went inside.

His mother, the old woman with the broken hearing aid, had made meatloaf. Her left foot had a stony corn—'plantar' something or other, she told her son. What else, he asked. 'Shingles,' she said.

He watched his girlfriend, who remained outside, watching the stop sign. She was swaying. The old woman with the hearing aid came over to look. Just then the redhead looked over at them and stared right into the old woman's eyes. Her arms billowed up, like both ends of a scarf in the wind. The son's hat flew up. The hair on all three of them shot up. The redhead began to walk in a slow curve. She slowly wound around herself in a spiral. The mother and son whirled even slower, flying up and spiraling around each other. The stop sign remained as it was.

The curator came to see me. He held my arm and talked and talked. His tongue got loose and lunged out of his mouth, becoming an attack dog. Then it became a fish flapping and thrashing around the room. I ducked to avoid his engorged, bucking tongue. His body was a kite being pulled by the tongue. His form was lashed and twirled around, as the tongue whipped the curator's helpless body. At one point it thumped him against the wall, knocking him unconscious. The tongue also slumped, then fluttered, and grew still.

Downtown I saw people running around in circles. Some people tore their own heads off and ran around in circles with their heads in their arms.

I had developed a coping mechanism called 'the envelope.' This was a technique wherein I folded in and sealed up on myself.

"You can't hide in there forever," Valkyrie would say.

I witnessed a woman sitting in a cloud. She combed her long hair and thought about all the stories she had been told as a child. Her mother had always said she could be whatever she wanted. But her family was disappointed that she chose to sit in the clouds. They had hoped she would choose a more practical vocation.

She no longer cared what they thought, however. She'd been sitting in the clouds for so long she had become detached. She snaked around between vaporous billows and watched the night sky. In the streets below, people were shooting at each other and running. The cloud woman witnessed houses on fire and people shouting through megaphones. She saw cats tearing upholstery and running down dark hallways, and then there were all the students who were getting sore necks and taking hostages.

"See," said her father, "now is the time for your generation to work hard, else we'll all die." Her mother took her to a place where she might be useful—a room where she was to lick and seal thousands of envelopes in order to help prevent the apocalypse.

They came back for her at the end of the day. She had failed to seal a single envelope. She lay sleeping on the floor. Her father collapsed into a chair and broke the leg. He hardly noticed the chair tilting over in his disappointment. His sobs woke the cloud woman up. "What happened?" she asked.

"Do you know we're all going to die because you're so lazy," her mother said. "It is your laziness that is causing the apocalypse." This made her so weary, the cloud woman passed out again. They left her drooling and twitching on the floor.

When she woke, she made a decision. She looked out of the window and saw clouds the exact shape of her lungs. She jumped out the window into the clouds.

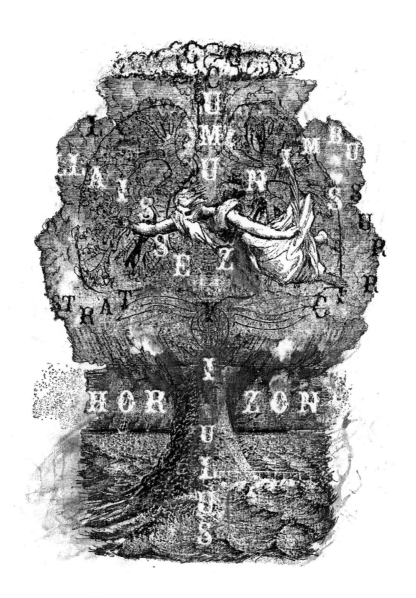

The cloud woman could see her parents. Her father would talk to her as if she was right in the room. "Why did you do it? You ungrateful creature, we counted on you." Her mother was on the phone trying to find people to seal envelopes. No one had time.

The cloud woman realized she needed to get even further away. She decided to fly right out of the galaxy into another galaxy. She soon forgot all about planet Earth.

I had grown use to the dank of the dump surrounding the lighthouse. But I was spending more and more time soaking in the smells at my uncle's in the city. People often stopped and stared at me on my perch, confided in me, or touched me as they passed.

One woman in particular had never wanted a child, but she lied and always said she wanted a child. She never had a child, but wouldn't stop lamenting the lack of a child that she never really wanted.

After a long hiatus, I delivered a one-hundred and seventy-eight page summary of my 'findings' that stated in its conclusion: *"Continuing growth in greenhouse gas emissions is leading to a higher standard of living that will result in a global utopia by the end of century."* The president quoted liberally from my report, hailing it as an objective docket.

Some chose to end their genetic line rather than risk bringing another lunatic into the world. "He could be the next Hitler," Some argued. "Or the next Einstein." This binary, the Hitler-Einstein dilemma, provided an inescapable deadlock for would-be breeders.

Inherited ambitions distracted people from the surreal encroachment of death. Some suspected they did not know their true desires. They were entrenched in so many contracts it would take the dexterity of a contortionist to escape.

A great squawking filled the air. A trumpeting battalion of frigate birds was heaving through the distant sky. They climbed into the clouds as one body. One sensed their collective weight, though the noise itself was transmitted on weightless sound waves, indicating precisely whence the flock came.

The girl whose father's head was attached to the top of hers had a revelation that she was the same as the world. She retreated to a well-trafficked corner to tell everyone. People gathered around. A quarter of the way through her speech she paused to take a breath. But the people who had gathered around thought she was done and clapped. Most of them clapped in the ordinary way. One kid had not been listening to the speech at all, but was wishing and pretending to be a monkey. When people started clapping, the girl pretending to be a monkey was startled out of her reverie. She started clapping too, but she clapped like this: on the first clap both arms went straight out in front of her, rigid like oars. On the second clap her hands hit hard and bounced off each other causing a ripple effect of several ever-diminishing claps. On the third clap she was unable to unclasp her hands and they wrestled to be free of each other; then a clap over the head; a clap to the side; and a clap right in front of her mother's face, which got her a slap.

Time would pass without my seeing or recording events. Some events I would have to imagine. The made-up events were sometimes more believable than actual events. The actual events were often difficult to believe.

I slept for a week. I awoke numb and looked out at the state. Things moved, had dimension, made sounds, slid right up to the surface, but could not poke through. Nothing was felt any longer, or known through the sense portals, despite the fact that every part of the body was designed for contact. Either the world, usually so flagrant, was camouflaged, or my surfaces were deteriorating. In any case, it was hidden.